THOMAS & FRIENDS™

The Big Race

When Thomas hears about a big race, he is eager to join in. Read along as you ride with Thomas on this exciting race around the Island of Sodor! You will know it is time to turn the page when you hear this sound.... Let's go!

Story Reader®

publications international, ltd.

As Henry finishes his last delivery, he tells Thomas about a race.

"I'm going to race Gordon, Neville, and Spencer to the end of the line and back," Henry says.

"Can I race too?" asks Thomas.

"Certainly, but remember, you are a small engine. You might not be able to keep up," Henry warns, as he chugs off.

Thomas pulls into Knapford Station and sees Gordon.

"I'm going to race with you today!" Thomas exclaims.

Gordon laughs. "This is a race for big engines like me," he says.

"I know," replies Thomas. "Small engines can race too!"

"All right, then, come along," says Gordon. "The race is about to begin."

Further down the track, Edward is hard at work shunting freight cars full of coal back and forth. Just then, he hears an engine steaming by. He looks up and sees Gordon racing along.

"Hello, Edward," says Gordon. "Not racing today?"

Edward explains that he would rather make deliveries than take part in the race.

"That's probably just as well," says Gordon. "You would have a hard time beating a powerful engine like me!"

"Good luck, Gordon," toots Edward, as Gordon continues on.

Gordon races quickly down the tracks until he reaches the farm.
Then he comes to a sudden stop. "Whoa, what's this?" he cries.

There is a cow munching on grass right in the middle of the tracks!
Gordon tries to get the cow to move.

Whoosh! Gordon releases steam from his funnel.

"Moo!" the cow responds, not moving.

Just then, Thomas comes puffing along. He chugs past the cow.

"PEEP! PEEP!" Thomas peeps loudly.

It works! Thomas' whistle startles the cow. The cow moves off the tracks. Thomas picks up speed.

"Thank you, Thomas!" says Gordon.

Thomas peeps goodbye as he steams back into the race.

Farther down the line, Neville races ahead of everyone. "Faster, faster!" he says to himself. Neville zooms past the docks toward a tunnel. He has never pushed himself this hard. Neville is very pleased with his speed.

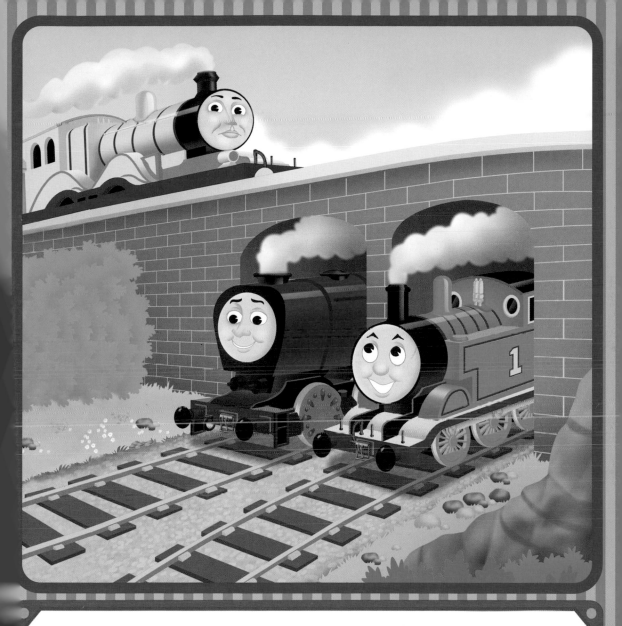

To Neville's surprise, when he comes out of the tunnel, there is an engine chugging next to him. It is Thomas!

"What a fast little engine you are!" Neville exclaims.

"This is fun!" peeps Thomas.

As the engines come around the corner, Neville speeds up and loses control.

"Oh no!" he cries, veering off the tracks.

Thomas stops. "Are you all right?" he asks.

"I'm fine," replies a disappointed Neville. "But I'm afraid I'm out of the race."

Thomas hears Harold and Molly in the distance and whistles loudly to get their attention. They come quickly to help.

"We'll have Neville back on the tracks in no time!" says Harold.

Knowing Neville has help, Thomas heads down the tracks once again.

Thomas races as fast as his wheels will carry him. Soon he catches up to Spencer.

"Thomas! Didn't expect to see you here!" says a very surprised Spencer.

"Sometimes small engines can be really fast too!" peeps Thomas.

"I can see that," replies Spencer, as Thomas speeds ahead.

Meanwhile, down the track, Henry sees Spencer and Thomas. Henry decides to take a shortcut. "I'll go this way to get around them!" Henry plans. He takes a side set of tracks up a big hill.

Thomas sees Henry veering off the main tracks and wants to warn him that Sir Topham Hatt told the engines not to use the tracks on the hill today.

Henry makes it up the hill quickly and down the other side even faster. He doesn't see the big puddle of mud until it is too late!

"Cinders and ashes!" Henry cries as he lands in the middle of the puddle. He tries moving forward. He tries moving backwards. He can't budge. Henry is stuck!

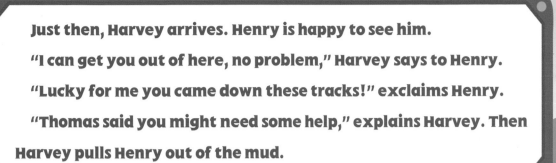

Just then, Harvey arrives. Henry is happy to see him.

"I can get you out of here, no problem," Harvey says to Henry.

"Lucky for me you came down these tracks!" exclaims Henry.

"Thomas said you might need some help," explains Harvey. Then Harvey pulls Henry out of the mud.

Back at the big race, Spencer has taken the lead. Thomas follows closely behind. Spencer is impressed. He must use all his effort to pull away from Thomas.

"See you at the finish line!" Spencer calls as he speeds away. Thomas may be fast, but Spencer is still faster.

Spencer turns around the bend—and screeches to a stop. The bridge ahead of him is out!

"Bust my boiler!" huffs Spencer. He looks at the broken tracks. There is no way for him to get across. He won't be able to finish the race after all.

The tracks on Thomas' side are clear. Thomas puffs by quickly and takes the lead again!

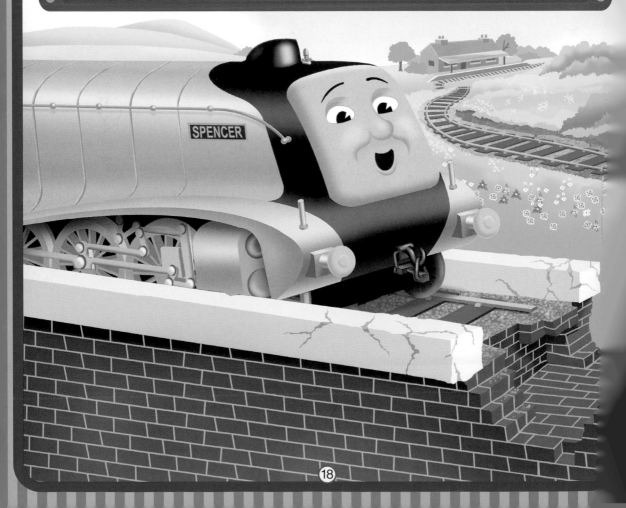

Spencer is sure the race is over when suddenly Thomas returns!

"Why did you come back?" asks Spencer. "You were going to win."

"You needed help," replies Thomas. "I brought workers and a load of bricks."

Thomas waits with Spencer while the workers fix the bridge.

When the bridge is complete, Thomas and Spencer head back to Knapford Station together.

Thomas pulls into the station just behind Spencer. He is the last engine to finish. As he pulls up to the platform, the engines cheer. "Why is everyone cheering?" Thomas asks.

"They're cheering for you!" replies Molly.

"The bigger engines said they could never have won the race, or even finished, if it hadn't been for your help!" Harvey explains.

Spencer, Neville, and Henry smile at Thomas and thank him.

"Still can't believe you raced us all," Gordon teases.

"You may be a small engine but you're very fast," Neville says kindly.

"And Really Useful, don't forget!" adds Thomas proudly.